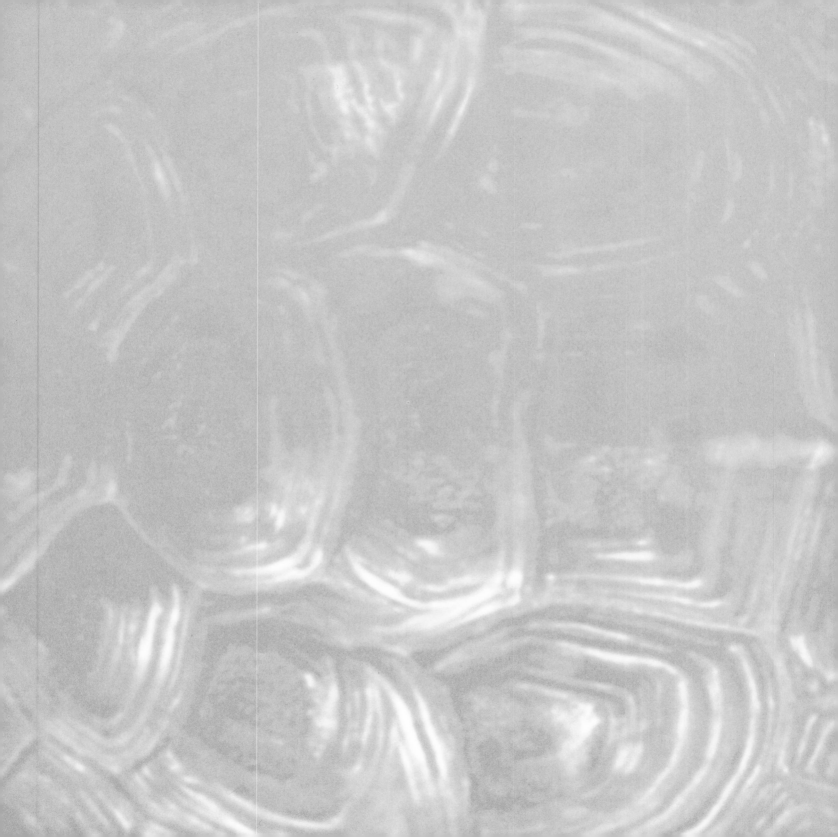

Chrissie's Shell

by Brooke Keith
Illustrations by Mary Bausman

To everyone who has ever felt empty…
  may God fill you to overflowing.
To everyone who has ever felt less than beautiful,
  look again…
    God made you *spectacular*.

For Chris, Alex, Brock, Emmy and Jack: Your shells have been filled so beautifully.
I'm so blessed to share my corner of the pond with you!

Warner Press Kids™
educate • nurture • inspire
www.warnerpress.org

79425017408

Library of Congress Cataloging-in-Publication Data

Keith, Brooke.
 Chrissie's shell / by Brooke Keith ; illustrated by Mary Bausman.
     p. cm.
 Summary: Chrissie the turtle compares herself unfavorably to all the
other animals in the forest but a conversation with God helps her
appreciate her own unique qualities.
 ISBN 978-1-59317-398-2
 [1. Turtles--Fiction. 2. Self-acceptance--Fiction. 3. Christian
life--Fiction.] I. Bausman, Mary, ill. II. Title.
 PZ7.K2525Ch 2010
 [E]--dc22
                          2010008999

Illustrations © 2010 by Warner Press

ISBN: 978-1-59317-398-2

Published by Warner Press, Inc, 1201 E. 5th Street, Anderson, IN 46012

Design Layout: Kevin Spear   Editors: Robin Fogle, Karen Rhodes

Printed in Mexico

Chrissie was a little invisible someone who lived in the deepest part of the biggest forest inside an, oh, so empty shell.

Lots of other someones lived in that same forest.
Real someones. Someones with big, moon-like eyes,
keeping watch from the tallest trees.

Someones with skinny, pink tails,
hanging upside down
from an oak branch.

Even fuzzy, green someones
with the magical ability
to turn into butterflies.

Chrissie liked to watch as all the interesting creatures passed by, and sometimes she would imagine what it would be like to be one.

Chrissie thought perhaps if she imagined hard enough she could become one...*for real.*

One sunny morning, Chrissie watched from her shell as a quick-footed field mouse scurried across the forest floor. He moved so swiftly that he looked like a furry little racecar!

And Chrissie was used to moving at a *much* slower pace than a furry racecar.

Once, Chrissie moved so slowly that she spotted a young blue lizard with a hurt leg, hobbling about on the forest's floor. She carried him right atop her back all the way home to his rock.

But it took a *whole* day to get that little critter home. And while the little lizard's mommy and daddy thanked Chrissie with warm hugs and slimy kisses, she knew that they probably wished a much faster creature had brought their baby home.

Sure, her slow pace allowed her to see the world around her with observant eyes—still, Chrissie wondered what it would be like to do the thing she could not do.

"I'm Chrissie, the speedy field mouse," she imagined. "My feet are fast like a million bunnies!" Chrissie sighed as she imagined herself racing through the grass and bobbing through the wildflowers.

She spent the morning deep inside a mousey daydream...

...until a wayward acorn fell from above, pinging right off the top of her shell! Chrissie peeked outside to see what was going on.

To her surprise, she saw a furry little squirrel looking in.

Had she done it? Had she become a field mouse? Chrissie took a look inside too, but she saw no fast feet, only darkness.

Her shell was empty.

So Chrissie tried again. This time she imagined she was a furry squirrel, climbing higher than all the other animals in the forest.

Oh, to be able to see the world from way up there!

Suddenly, as Chrissie was gazing way *up* to the treetops, she saw a tiny blue egg falling *down* fast. It landed smack dab in the middle of the pond!

Chrissie swam down to get it, but by that time, the little blue egg was soaked. If she had been a squirrel, maybe she could have leaped right down from those tall, tall trees and rescued that little egg before it even touched the cold water!

Sure, Chrissie
was a terrific
dip-n-diver, but still
she imagined what it
would be like to do the
thing she could not do.

"I'm Chrissie, the highest-
climbing squirrel in all the land! My
furry feet can take me up, up, up into the
tallest trees!" Chrissie tried hard to think as
many squirrel-like thoughts as she could, and she spent
the afternoon deep inside a squirrelly daydream.

Later, with the moon as her guide,
Chrissie checked to see if she had become
a real squirrel.

No furry body.

No fluffy tail.

No sharp teeth.

Just as before, she found her shell was empty.

The next day she noticed a tiny hedgehog, slowly passing by.
His spikes looked so strong! His prickles so ferocious!

Oh, to be as strong as a spiky hedgehog!

"I'm Chrissie, the strongest critter in all the forest!
I can spike up my shell with the power of a million prickles!"

Taking a deep breath,
Chrissie tried *really* hard to
puff out those prickles she
was sure she had created!

Before Chrissie could finish her
hedgehoggy daydream, she began to feel
just a little light-headed. Then a wayward raindrop
plinked down upon her shell. As the rain fell around her,
she noticed a little flutter-by firefly that was caught in the storm.
She invited it to fly beneath her shell for comfort from the rain.

As the storm passed, the firefly fluttered
on its way. Chrissie checked once more to see
if her daydream had worked...but no,
her shell was...

still empty.

Chrissie felt very sad.

"God," whispered Chrissie.
"If you're up there, could you
make me into a real someone?"

"A real someone?" asked God.

"Yes, God. My shell is empty. You
must have forgotten to fill it."

"Hmm, an *empty* shell, you say?"

"Yes," said Chrissie.
"Could you make me into
a bear? Wouldn't a bear
look nice inside my shell?"

"Well," replied God,
"a bear might be a little too
chubby to fit into such a
small space."

"Maybe you're right," said Chrissie. "How about a bunny instead? I would make a very good bunny."

"A bunny?" questioned God. "A cotton tail might look kind of silly, fluffing out the back of a shell."

"Yes, but..." Chrissie stammered.

"Chrissie," interrupted God. "Are you sure you haven't missed something? Look inside your shell again."

And she did.

But she *still* saw nothing. Her shell was just as empty as ever!

"I told you. There's no one in there!" cried Chrissie.

"Yes, there is," assured God. "There is a very smart, very creative, very wonderful little someone in there. I know. I made her.

"This special person is not quick like a field mouse. She never will be. I made her slow enough to help little lost lizards.

Unlike a squirrel, she is not a steady climber. She's a sensational swimmer instead. Look in the trees, Chrissie. Do you see that nesting bluebird? She is sitting on the very egg your swimming saved!

And you may not be prickly like a hedgehog, but I gave you a shell to keep you safe and warm...one that can help protect others too.

Don't you see? It's not what you can *do* that matters, Chrissie, it's who you *are* inside. I didn't need another anything else in the world. All I needed was a *you*. And your shell is not as empty as you think. Come over to the pond. I have something to show you."

Chrissie's heart was sad as she walked slowly to the edge of the pond.

She would never be a running field mouse, never a brave, treetop-gazing squirrel, never an oh, so strong hedgehog. No bear. No bunny.

What good was an empty shell?

Flopping down, she watched
as a lone star twinkled in the
distance and moonlight fell
across the pond.

It created a picture across the water.

Chrissie looked down, down into the quiet depths of the pond. Looking back at her was someone she had never noticed before.

"Isn't she lovely?" asked God.

"Why, yes!" said Chrissie. "She is. But who is she?"

"Why, that's you, *little turtle*. That's *you*."

That night Chrissie lay awake for hours, peering across the moonlit pond. She watched in amazement as both the reflection of a real—life someone and the echoes of a thousand twinkling stars rippled on the waves.

And then?

Chrissie curled up inside her not-so-empty shell and went to sleep,

where she dreamed of being...herself.

I praise you because I am...wonderfully made. PSALM 139:14 (NIV)